THE HAWTHORNE BLOW

For information, or to order additional copies,
please contact:

Beacon Publishing Group
P.O. Box 41573 Charleston, S.C. 29423
800.817.8480| beaconpublishinggroup.com

Publisher's catalog available by request.

ISBN-13: 978-1-949472-25-7

ISBN-10: 1-949472-25-7

Published in 2021. New York, NY 10001.

First Edition. Printed in the USA.

THE HAWTHORNE BLOW

BY MATTHEW HELLMAN

CHAPTER ONE

What the hell is down there? Sam Halvorsen thought. His pole was bent over, nearly in half, the tip pointing at the glare of the July sun reflecting off the sparkling Lake Superior water. He throttled his boat to neutral and shut the engine down.

He was pleased with himself for having the foresight to take a vacation day on this beautiful July Friday. The fish were really hitting. Grabbing the pole out of the downrigger he gave a tentative tug, sure he'd somehow snagged something on the bottom. To his pleasant surprise, something on the other end tugged back.

Sam had barely started reeling when the rod was nearly yanked out of his hands. What the hell could do that? Nothing in this lake. Whatever was down there couldn't be like anything he'd ever caught before. He peered suspiciously at the line where it disappeared into the depths. The line danced as he felt another weighty tug. He looked around at the surrounding lake, searching for witnesses to what must be a gigantic fish. He saw only a vacant shoreline a half-mile to his right, and a vast expanse of nothing but blue to his left.

"Wow. This one must be huge," he said out loud to himself. His pulse quickened, but with patience wrought from years of fishing the big lake, Sam resumed reeling in the catch. Over his shoulder he located his net, doubting it was sufficient to the task. Another big pull made him wonder if *he* was sufficient to the task. Then, without so much as a furious counter-fight, the line went slack. *Dammit.* Disheartened, he continued to reel, needing to see if the fish had just escaped or if it had snapped the line. But he could feel there was still something there, something still on the hook, but it wasn't fighting at all. The line draped through the air, the tension in it gone. Sam wound faster until he felt the line tighten again. The thing he had hooked seemed to be swimming straight up at the boat.

Able to see through tens of feet of the crystal-clear water, Sam gasped at the shape emerging from the depths. His heart quickened and a warm flush pooled in his cheeks. He cringed as the diver broke the surface, Sam's lure hooked high between the shoulders of the black dry suit. He dropped the pole and offered a hand.

Seething green eyes glared up at him through the mask as the diver accepted Sam's assistance and climbed onto the back of his boat. He blushed doubly hard now, realizing that this was, quite obviously, a female diver. She spat out her mouthpiece, pulled off her mask and drew back her hood, revealing shoulder length, chestnut hair. Her fair skin accentuated the blue of her lips. It was Heather something-or-other. He'd seen her around town before and had never gotten up the nerve to talk to her. This wasn't the kind of introduction he'd imagined.

"What the hell are you doing?" She waved her arm in an arc around the peacefully rolling water, an old, wicked knife in her hand. "You don't troll over the top of a diver down "

She paused as she looked at the empty lake around them and the shoreline. "Sign," she finished. Her face a mask of worry, she asked, "Where's my sign? Where's my boat?"

Not feeling quite so foolish now, as there was no floating 'diver-down' sign, and no boat, Sam relaxed.

"Let me unhook you before you get hurt," Sam said. He reached to turn her around and she swatted his hands away. "Relax. I just want to take the hook out."

She gazed at him intensely for a moment then turned her back, keeping her head looking over her shoulder. Sam patiently worked the hook loose, doing his best not to rip the dry suit more than necessary, though it was already ruined. "There."

"What happened to my boat? It was right here," she said, pointing with the vicious blade still in hand.

An uneasy feeling settled in Sam's stomach. "You aren't a pirate, are you?" he asked, tipping his head toward her knife, testing a grin.

"I didn't steal anyone's boat." It sounded like an accusation, making Sam bristle.

"Really?" Now Sam's voice had an edge.

"Sorry." Sam watched her trying to calm down. "My boat was right here."

"It isn't now. Would you put the knife down?" he insisted.

She nodded. "I found this on the wreck," she said. She lay the antique dagger on the seat next to her. After regaining some semblance of civility, she offered her hand. "I'm Heather Case, by the way."

"Sam Halvorsen," he replied. Her hand was cold as ice from being in the frigid water. He met her eyes again. This time somewhat taken by their beauty. Quickly, he looked away.

"Found that on the wreck? You mind?"

Heather looked him over and finally nodded. He reached down and took the knife, turning it over in his hands, examining the handle and blade. Nothing fancy. Just looked like a work knife, like something any sailor would carry on a ship covered with lines and sails.

Somewhere in the depths below and aft was the wreck of the Hawthorne, sunk here sometime in the mid-1800s, taking one of Sam's ancestors with it. Savvy locals knew it was a good place for fish. But because it was only about sixty feet deep, it was attractive for anyone crazy enough to dive in the fifty-degree water.

Sam personally felt that anyone diving in Lake Superior was either extremely hardy or completely nuts. Heather didn't seem nuts, but Sam didn't like to rush to judgment.

A sound made him look back towards the wreck. Heather heard it too, her head snapping to peer out at the water. He tossed the knife back on the seat.

They watched as the clear, cold water above the wreck of the Hawthorne frothed and roiled, as if someone had turned on pumps to a huge hot tub. He regarded Heather but saw her brow creased with the same confusion he felt. The water continued in that fashion for several more seconds before finally settling down.

"What was that all about?" Sam asked.

"Beats me," Heather answered. "Maybe something in the wreck settled and let loose a bunch of trapped air."

"What'd you do down there, break it?" He let a sly smile tug at the corners of his mouth.

"No. I didn't even touch the thing." She looked at Sam and he noticed her grin when she realized he was chiding her.

Sam turned to look north. Some 160 miles distant was the Canadian shore. But near the limit of his vision he saw what he was looking for.

"There's a boat out there. Your pilot just decide to leave you here and do some fishing of his own?"

Heather squinted out at the water. "I don't have a pilot. Just me. It was anchored."

Sam considered her for a moment. She was young, late twenties, maybe a year or two older than Sam. Obviously confident enough to dive, but dumb enough to do it alone? Why would she lie about having a pilot? The likelihood of her being nuts was starting to increase. When he was approaching the wreck, trolling, he was sure he'd seen a boat heading out to deep water, slowly but not just drifting. It had been too far away to be able to hear a motor, but Sam figured it had to have been under power to cover the distance it had by the time he arrived.

"How long were you down there?" Sam asked.

"Half-hour."

"Boat went a long way by itself. You sure it was anchored?"

Heather scowled. "I know how to anchor a boat."

Sam wondered about that. "Okay. Let's go get it."

Sam fired up the engine and headed out to retrieve Heather's runaway vessel. It had drifted a good mile-and-a-half from the wreck. Upon reaching it, Heather stepped into her smaller craft and then reached across to tie the two boats together. Sam climbed over and found her anchor line on the bow, its length snaking limply in the water.

"There's no anchor on here," he said as he pulled the rope in. "Are you sure you had it tied tight?"

"Yeah. I've used that anchor for a couple of years. Knot was solid."

The frayed end of the rope emerged from the water, the line being well short of being able to reach the bottom where Heather had been diving. Sam eyed the fibers, then stared at Heather.

"Looks like it's been cut," he announced.

"What?" She snatched the shortened line and examined it. She looked at Sam, eyes narrowing.

Sam retrieved the knife Heather had brought up from the depths and tested its edge.

"Could you have cut the line accidentally? This knife is still pretty sharp."

Heather took a deep breath and let it out in a huff before answering. "No. I didn't accidentally cut it."

"Well, something cut your line. And..." he broke off when he noticed the terrified look on her face as she looked past him. She pointed towards shore.

"Go! Go!" she yelled.

Sam spun around and saw a gargantuan swell rolling at them from the area of the wreck. He'd never seen such a massive wave on Lake Superior, and never one defying nature as it traveled out to sea. It was like a leviathan's wake, swelling up as a submerged monster swam to crush them. He jumped back over into his boat and cut one line connecting his boat to Heather's as she cast off the other line. She ran to her controls and cranked the ignition but the motor sputtered stubbornly as they drifted apart.

The guys at the repair shop always came to Sam when the diagnostic computers were not reporting error codes from the engines or were giving some code unrelated to the problem. He could always troubleshoot the tough cases. It was, he told the other guys, because he knew how engines worked. Computers don't, they just monitor sensors. In normal circumstances, Sam would take a look at her engine and have it running in a matter of minutes. But these were hardly normal circumstances.

"Hurry up," Sam yelled. He looked at the massive swell of water rushing at them, only about four hundred yards distant. If that wave hit them broadside, it'd swamp both boats for sure and the icy water would send them into hypothermia before anyone could find them. He tossed the knife under the passenger side dashboard and tightened his lifejacket.

Heather yelled as she tried in vain to start her boat.

"Forget it. Get over here!" He'd left his motor running.

With slight hesitation, Heather dove into the water, her momentum propelling her through the cold twelve-foot gap. She surfaced with arms uplifted and, like they'd rehearsed a well-timed routine, Sam reached down with both hands, grabbed her wrists and yanked her up over the gunwale. In a not so well rehearsed move, Sam dumped her on the floor of his boat, jumped to the throttle and punched it. He looked to his left, in the direction of the oncoming mountain of water.

Heather clambered into the passenger's seat and braced herself. "We aren't going to make it," Heather announced, staring at the wall of cold death.

Sam frowned. "Hold on." He pulled the wheel hard to the left, pointing his 22-foot boat directly at the wave.

"Oh shit," Heather said as the bow started to climb.

Sam saw tears form in Heather's eyes just before he turned to see the bow of his boat bite into the crushing wall of water.

CHAPTER TWO

Lily Swanson looked at her little flower garden. It needed fertilizer and insecticide. She loved it because flowers don't judge. They just absorb attention and radiate beauty and peace. They were nothing like the miserable fiends at school. As much as she hated the kids at school, she hated the Japanese beetles more. She threw a glance at Sam's house across the street. She wished he could give her a ride to the hardware store, but she'd seen him leaving with his fishing pole, no doubt heading out on the big lake all day. He was so nice and friendly. So mature. Of course. She wished there were some boys who weren't such idiots. And girls who weren't such catty bitches.

And she wished she were normal. But she wasn't and, once again, the whole school knew about her. Her family had moved here four years ago, hoping to give her a new start in a new school. The bullying had become unmanageable where they had been living, down-state.

After a good start, things had started up again. Even though her last episode had been two years ago, no one forgot. Kids don't forget a weirdo. At sixteen, she found herself with precious few friends. None, to be exact. There were one or two who finally didn't act like she had leprosy, but no one who wanted to be seen talking to her. Silly Lily.

There was one boy who showed promise. Jake Henderson. He was good looking, and almost always polite to her. In fact, he had never called her Silly Lily. He played football and had a shy smile and broad shoulders. She hoped that maybe he would ask her to prom.

It was a terrifying thought. It was hope beyond hope. Consciously she beat the thought down, not wanting to be disappointed in the end. But deep in the recesses of her mind, a match-light of hope in the never-ending dark void of space flickered in defiance. Jake might ultimately grow to like her.

And Jake worked at the hardware store.

Which is why Lily really wanted someone to go with her. Her parents were working. And if Jake saw her with someone else...

But Sam was out fishing.

And she really needed fertilizer and insecticide. So, against her better judgment, she hopped on her bike and set off for the store.

Water crashed over the bow of Sam's boat, the wave breaking just as the craft started to stall at the crest. Sam was driven into his seat by the weight of the water. The little boat jolted as the water hammered into the transom. He glanced to his left and saw Heather spitting water as she blinked at him. All at once they pitched forward as they flew down the back side of the swell, water rushing around their feet. Sam expected to see a huge trough in the water behind the wave, but to his surprise the surface was only mildly disrupted, letting the boat glide down instead of being propelled bow-first into the water like an air-launched torpedo.

When the boat settled, Sam pulled back on the throttle and checked behind them. The wave was gone. It was as if it had never existed. Heather's boat was gone too.

Ankle-deep in cold water, he flipped on the pumps, hoping they hadn't been damaged in the jarring deluge. Hearing the hum of the motors, he looked over the side, pleased to see a jet of water shooting forth. He noted that the boat sat about a foot lower in the water. He set a course for shore, slow until enough water had been pumped out to take it up to full speed.

Heather looked like she had when he first

pulled her from the water, dripping wet and knife in hand. She was staring at the empty water, trembling.

"My boat is gone. My gear..."

"You had insurance, right?"

She nodded. "Still..."

"We're alive," Sam said. "Somehow. What was that?" he asked.

She shook her head, still scanning the blue expanse where her boat had been. There wasn't even flotsam. "Rogue wave?"

Sam looked at the antiquity that she'd brought up from the wreck of the Hawthorne. "Maybe you're some kind of Indiana Jones, stealing artifacts and drudging up old curses and booby traps."

She considered the knife, then shifted her gaze to Sam, scowling. "That's ridiculous. Let's get to shore."

The water gone from the floor of the boat, Sam steadily increased the throttle until he felt the craft handle normally. Then he maxed out his speed and headed for the marina, his mind trying to decipher what had happened. Looking back, he thought he saw a big sailing ship, enshrouded in a feathery mist, floating over Heather's sunken boat. When he blinked, it was gone.

He was working. With school out, Jake worked a lot more. He'd even said 'hello' when Lily walked into the store. 'Hello'. To her! Having had her mind blown just a bit, she walked up and down several aisles, trying to remember why she was there. Could it be he didn't see her as a weirdo? He was handsome. And polite. And he had a group of friends, so he wasn't a loner like her, so he didn't *need* to be friendly.

"Can I help you find something?"

Jake!

Lily focused on the merchandise on the shelf in front of her. Garbage bags. "I was just seeing what garbage bags you have," she answered. Then, "I don't need these, right now, though." She shot him a weak smile. "But I do need... um... for, ah... flowers! For flowers... for bugs... on flowers..."

"Insecticide?" Jake finished for her.

"Yes! And fertilizer," she added with a note of triumph.

"It's right over here." The dashingly handsome and charming young man led Lily to aisle five. Her new favorite aisle.

"Great. Thank you," Lily said. She took a bottle of spray and pretended to read the label which may as well have been written in Chinese. Actually, the part she was looking at was written in Chinese.

"Fertilizer is right down there," Jake said. He pointed at the bottom shelf, near the end of the row.

"Let me know if there is anything else I can help you with." He smiled and walked away.

He smiled! And walked away. He didn't run. So far, so good. She took a deep breath, trying to focus on the task at hand, so she'd look normal. After considering several different bug sprays, she settled on one and then grabbed her tried-and-true fertilizer.

Now to complete the purchase. She strode to the front of the store, expertly navigating around mid-floor displays of lightbulbs, past precariously positioned rakes, dodging an oblivious old lady. The register and Jake were in plain view, waiting.

"You all set?" Jake asked.

She placed the items on the counter. "Yep." *Keep it simple*, she thought.

He scanned the items on the computer and provided the total. Ten dollars and 58 cents.

Lily took out her wallet and retrieved two five-dollar bills and presented them to Jake. "Oh. I have some change," she said. She dug out exactly 58 cents. How impressive she must look, putting on a display of financial acumen. She reached out to place the coins in Jake's calloused, yet no doubt, tender, hand. As she did their hands touched.

Black shadows formed a circle around her vision, closing in on the image of her and Jake's hands like a contracting camera aperture. *No!* She screamed in her mind. *Not now!*

The sky was dark, bleak and cold. Wind whipped wet, stinging snow into the faces of the three men who stood near... what? A tree? The men were soaked, shivering and clearly frightened. One of the men held a knife out in front of him, keeping the other two at bay. They were dressed in coats, hats and gloves, appropriate for the swirling snow and wet freezing rain that fell on them. She could hear part of what the men were saying over the howling blow of the wind.

"...wrong with you? We can...", from one of the two. *He turned as he spoke and Lily thought she was looking at her neighbor, Sam.*

"I'm going to... think we can all... crazy," from the knife wielder.

The men stumbled around as though drunk. The third man turned in Lily's direction. Jake? It looked like Jake, but older. What was he doing?

Then she saw, rather than heard, a name: Melville.

The knife flashed forward, catching Jake in the side, piercing deeply before getting yanked out again, a spray of blood mixing with the wet precipitation. Jake crumpled to the ground, his eyes fading as his life drained away in the sloshing waters.

"Are you okay?" Jake's voice. "Lily?"

His voice sliced through the cold fog that gripped Lily's mind. She opened her eyes.

"You fainted, or had a seizure or something," he told her. "Do you need me to call an ambulance?"

She'd had another damned vision. Why? Why now? It'd been two years. She thought they had stopped. Now, at the worst possible time, they start up again. When she finally has a chance to convince one boy that she is normal, she freaks out. Then she noticed the warm wetness in the crotch of her jeans, her bladder having released while she was out.

Suppressing a sob, she jumped up and ran out of the store, leaving her fertilizer, insecticide and Jake behind.

CHAPTER THREE

Emerson Lintela loved fishing on Lake Superior. People not familiar with it were always surprised to learn that it had a surface area comparable to South Carolina and the liquid in it could cover all of North and South America in a foot of water. Because of its astronomical size, Lintela had learned to respect the big lake. But he lived for days like this, when the sun was high and warm, but the air close to the surface of the water was cool and refreshing. And the water looked glass-clear until you looked to the horizon, then it was the most indescribable blue imaginable.

The air rushed through his sandy hair as he powered his boat to the next, and probably last, fishing spot. With the morning having gone so well, he would likely fill his limit over the old wreck.

He spotted another boat racing in his direction, the white spray of the water breaking away from its bow as it approached. They would pass a couple of hundred yards off his starboard side. As it got closer, Emerson thought he recognized the vessel. Yep. That was Sam Halvorsen's boat. But it looked like there were two people in it and the one looked like a woman. Suddenly, the oncoming boat swerved and took a heading that would put it directly in Emerson's path.

"What the hell you doin'?" Emerson muttered. He eased back on his throttle.

Halvorsen continued to drive right at the old fisherman, finally forcing Emerson to cut his speed to a full stop and shut the engine off. He saw Sam's passenger waving her arms over her head.

Who've you got with you, Sam? he thought. He smiled and waved as they approached, but he noticed a stern look on the young man's face. Finally, Sam reined in his own boat and the bow dropped as it settled into the water, the wake dying as it fanned out and set Emerson's boat to rocking.

"Hey Emerson. I hope you aren't going out to the wreck," Sam said.

"Sure am. Don't want me catching your fish?"

"Something weird is going on out there. We nearly got capsized by this huge wave that came out of nowhere."

Emerson squinted at the couple. He thought he recognized the woman. Maybe someone his wife had known from work or something. She had a frightened look about her.

"A wave?" Emerson asked

"It sank my boat," the woman said.

"You okay?"

The woman nodded.

"And the water was kind of, like, boiling or something. Maybe the wreck is unstable. I'd stay away from it for a couple of days."

Emerson considered Sam's words. He'd always known the young man to be normal. Even intelligent. He was a wiz with motors. Boiling water? What had they been up to out there? This sounded like some drug induced hallucination. That would explain why Sam had driven on a collision course with him. Sam knows better than that.

"I'll keep my eyes open," Emerson said.

"No. Really. I don't think you should go out there," the woman said.

Emerson nodded as he cranked up the engine. "If I see anything dangerous, I'll high-tail it out of there." With a wave he pulled forward until he could accelerate to full speed and get to his fishing spot. When he glanced back, he saw Sam's boat cruising back towards the marina.

Damned drugs sure made people squirrelly.

He drove for ten more minutes before casting his line out and letting it drop until he felt the sinker bounce against the bottom. He set the pole in the pole-holder and set his motor on a suitable trolling speed. When he went past the wreck, the lure would be perfectly positioned to attract fish in the sixty-foot water, shallow by Lake Superior standards.

Emerson sat at the steering wheel and watched the pole tip, periodically looking around for other boats or floating hazards. But his eyes always returned to the pole. When he happened to look north, where only water should be visible all the way to the distant horizon, he noticed a dark cloud. Not high in the sky, or immeasurably distant, but low and close, as though it clung to the lake. He judged it to be about three miles away. Except for its threatening gray color, it didn't look like a storm cloud. More like angry fog. Or smoke. But just a patch. It reminded him of the cloud of dust that clung to, and followed around, the little guy named 'Pigpen' in the Peanuts comics. The unusual fog hadn't been there just a few minutes ago.

The sound of his fishing pole rattling in the pole-holder snatched his attention. He grabbed the rod and gave it a hard tug. He was rewarded by the familiar sporadic yanking of a fish. Reeling in his catch, he turned and looked at the dark cloud. It was closer. A lot closer. Maybe only a mile at this point. It was unnerving to look at. Once this fish was up, he was heading in the opposite direction. The tension on his line changed from the frantic fight he expected, to a steady, dull drag. Emerson looked at the concentric circles that radiated from where his line pierced the surface of the water, his brow furrowed. He was sure he hadn't lost the fish because he could still feel the weight of it when he lifted his pole tip. But it had completely given up fighting.

Glancing at the imposing storm cloud, or whatever the hell it was, he quickened his retrieval, just wanting to get the fish up, throw it in the bottom of the boat and get gone. Finally, the fish came up over the back of the boat. It hung limp from the lure, completely lifeless. Emerson dropped the fish and pole and leaped to the engine controls, unable to look away from the fog that was now only two hundred yards away and closing fast. He turned the key and heard the motor struggle to life.

One hundred yards. The stench of decay assailed his nostrils.

Emerson pushed the throttle lever down and the engine sputtered, nearly choking out before revving up and propelling the craft forward.

Within the gray mist, Emerson thought he saw the bow of a ship coming right at him. As he sped away, the shrouded vessel changed course, looking as though it meant to ram him. He grabbed his marine radio mike and called in a desperate plea, saying he was about to be rammed by a ship.

Then the cloud overtook him.

And never in his life had he felt that cold.

CHAPTER FOUR

After exchanging numbers, Sam checked to make sure his boat was securely tied in the slip and headed home. Heather was off to report her sunken boat and its location to the Coast Guard.

Sam wasn't sure what had happened today. The roiling water and then that huge wake, he considered it a wake and not just a wave, were nothing he'd ever seen or even heard of before.

He was sure it must have had something to do with the wreck, seeing as how they were so close to it. The bubbling, churning water must have been the result of the wreck settling and setting loose trapped air or gas. Heather must have touched something down there.

But that wake that swamped and sunk Heather's boat was another matter. Since when do waves originate out of nowhere and head away from shore? It had reminded Sam of the wake created by a big fish pursuing a shallow running lure, but hundreds of times larger. There were reports dating back into the 1800s of huge sea creatures in the lake. But there was no evidence of such a thing today. And he doubted even the ocean's blue whale could create a wake like that.

Chastising himself for considering such fanciful ideas, he struggled to come up with an explanation. Maybe one of the big cliff faces had broken away, like a chunk shearing off a glacier, and that caused the big wave? They hadn't noticed any significant difference in the shoreline, but then they weren't really looking.

That had to be it. There was no other logical explanation.

It was nearing dinner time when he finally pulled into his driveway. Lily was sitting on his front porch looking forlorn. *Oh no. Now what happened,* he thought. After the day he'd had, Sam wasn't in the mood for comforting his neighbor's insecure teenage girl. But she didn't seem to have anyone her own age to talk to, and there were some things kids didn't want to discuss with their parents. He sighed as he got out of his truck.

"Hey," he said.

Lily looked up, her eyes bloodshot from crying. "Hey, Sam."

"You don't look happy. What's going on?"

"I had another...event." She cast her eyes down and wiped her nose.

"I thought they'd stopped."

She nodded. "Me too. But..."

Sam sat next to her on the porch step. "What happened?"

Lily related what happened at the hardware store, even going so far as to let Sam in on her hopes that she and Jake might hit it off. She concluded with, "I peed myself." And the tears started again.

Sam hoped she didn't see him cringe. Wetting her pants might be tough for a teenage boy to look past. But he couldn't let her dwell on it. "I'm sure Jake knows that it was not something under your control. I certainly do, and he seems like a bright kid." He saw a feeble spark of hope light in Lily's eyes. "What was the vision? Do you want to talk about it?"

Lily squared herself to him, wiped the tears away, licked her lips and nodded. "That's actually why I really wanted to talk to you."

Sam frowned. He'd never seen Lily so authoritative.

"I saw you and Jake in my vision. Someone was trying to stab you."

"Really?" Sam asked. He was more than a little disconcerted that she had seen him in her mind's eye. She'd never told him one of her visions, just that she'd had them a few years back and it had caused her issues at school because she went into a trancelike state and occasionally fell over as a result. The events had earned her the nickname 'Silly Lily'. He had never really believed she had visions, but rather some type of seizure or such. But here she was telling him something quite specific.

"You may have been on a boat or something, there was a lot of water, and maybe a mast? Anyway, this guy had a knife and he stabbed Jake with it, but Jake looked older than he is now. You maybe a little bit too."

"That's pretty scary," Sam conceded. He didn't want to belittle Lily, but it sounded more like a waking dream than anything to be concerned about. Then an image of Heather holding the knife she'd found skittered through his mind. He forced a smile.

Lily regarded Sam for a moment. "You don't believe me," she said.

"No. I believe you. I just don't know what it means. It could be anything."

"Remember when Bill Remer got killed by that drunk driver two years ago?" she said.

Sam nodded.

"I saw that before it happened. Those were what my visions were about." She squinted as she looked down, mouth tightening. "I think something bad is going to happen to you and Jake."

"Don't worry too much, okay. I hardly know Jake and I can't imagine we'll be together on a ship anytime soon. Especially one with a murderer on board."

Lily shook her head. "That's not how it works. It's not always literal. I saw Bill get crushed by a tree." She met his eyes. "Please be careful. You're the only friend I have."

Sam exhaled through a smile. "I will. I'll be extra careful."

She stood up. "Thanks." She started back across the lawn towards her own house, then turned. "And let me know if anything weird happens. Okay?"

Anything weird? Like the lake churning and a huge wave coming from out of nowhere? "I will." He waved good-bye and went into his house. He slumped his back against the closed door. What happened out on the lake definitely fit into the category of 'weird'. And the possible explanations for it didn't feel right. They felt desperate.

Not that Lily's vision explained anything. Two years ago he'd thought the gossip about her having 'psychic episodes' was some twisted cover for her having insecurity. He knew the kids picked on her so he always made sure to be warm and friendly. He didn't want her to go the same route as Maggie. Since that time, he kind of came to think of Lily as a little sister. So, he knew, when she had looked him dead in the eye and told him about her vision, she believed what she was saying.

Sam didn't consider himself close-minded, but ESP, UFOs, bigfoot, ghosts, all that weird crap was just fodder to entertain the mind. It wasn't real. At least he didn't think it was. It was obvious that Lily not only believed in the paranormal, but she believed she was experiencing it. Sam was much happier with his mechanic's world; things had a cause and effect that you could see or calculate with science.

Apparently, Sam's hard-wired science world and Lily's paranormal world had just collided. He hoped it didn't leave a mess.

When did Lily have her vision, relative to what happened to Heather and him? Could what she saw have anything to do with their almost getting capsized? No. The vision was of three men, not a man and a woman. But she said it wasn't something to take literally. Maybe the danger she saw to him was the big wave trying to drown him and the threat was already past.

Or maybe there was a stabbing in his future.

CHAPTER FIVE

Heather plodded into her little two-bedroom house, dropping what was left of her diving gear just inside the door. Her meeting with the Coast Guard had gone predictably badly. The only good to come of it was that she realized explaining how her boat sunk to the insurance rep was something to prepare for, because the Coast Guard wasn't buying it. 'Rogue wave' wasn't in their vocabulary when talking waters a half-mile offshore in Lake Superior. She needed to have what's-his-name...Sam, make a written witness statement. Great.

She tossed her newly acquired antique knife on the table and collapsed into a chair.

What the hell had happened, anyway? First the boat gets cut loose and drifts away. A long ways away. Then the water boils. Then the massive wave almost kills them and sinks her boat. The best thing to happen was when she got hooked by Sam's fishing line. And that sucked. At least he was easy on the eyes and not an outright jerk like most of the guys she met. This was truly the weirdest day she'd ever had. And as an eighth-grade English teacher, she'd had some weird days, though usually in a funny, entertaining way. Today was terrifying.

The random wave was the most disturbing. Where had that come from, and how? Had it come from the direction of shore, by the wreck? Nothing made any sense. Not yet. Things always have a logical explanation, however elusive that may be.

She turned on her TV. The local news was just starting.

The lead story was that the Coast Guard received a panicked call from a boater on Lake Superior with news of a 'ghost ship'. Heather turned her full attention on the story. The news anchor went on to say that shortly after 4:00 PM, the Coast Guard received a radio transmission from a fisherman who said he was about to be rammed by a ghost ship in a heavy fog. The transmission ended abruptly and in a manner that raised officials' concerns for the safety of the boater. Rescue boats from both Dollar Bay and Marquette were sent out and several other fishing boats that heard the distress call responded as well. When the rescuers arrived, they found the fisherman frozen to death and no evidence of a collision.

Heather shook her head, not sure she'd heard the newsman correctly. As if he knew the listeners would want to hear that again, he repeated that the man had been found frozen to death, on a warm sunny day in the middle of July.

Heather felt a chill settle on her skin as the on-scene reporter, standing on the shores of Lake Superior, droned on in the background. How does a guy freeze to death on a 75-degree day under a blazing sun? Did she wake up in Weirdville, USA this morning?

"...the Hawthorne Blow," she heard a local say to the reporter. That got her attention. The Hawthorne Blow was an icy and early November storm back in the 1800s that was responsible for sinking the ore ship, the Hawthorne. Old mariners would sometimes refer to the phenomenon of freakishly cold weather striking ships out on the lake as the Hawthorne Blow. Saying the phrase out loud unsettled sailors who would not speak of the dark portents associated with "the Blow". The field reporter concluded his report saying that because the victim had been found in close proximity to the wreck of the Hawthorne, locals had already dredged up the old curse.

With a curse of her own, Heather shut off the TV. Who was the poor guy? They hadn't released his name yet. Was it that guy she and Sam had warned when they were on their way in?

The phone rang. The landline's electronic vibrato shattering her thoughts.

"Hello,"

"Heather? This is Sam Halvorsen. Did you see the news tonight?"

Heather rubbed her forehead, eyes closed. "Yeah."

"I think they were talking about Emerson Lintela, the guy we talked to. They say he froze to death? What the hell?"

Her lips pulled into a frown. Emerson! He'd looked familiar but she didn't know him well. She knew his wife, a retired teacher. Such a sweet woman, and she'd always talked with adoring fondness about her husband. Heather slumped into a chair and dropped her forehead into a hand. Life wasn't fair. "I don't know," she said.

"Something is going on," Sam continued. "I know it sounds weird, and I was just joking about booby-traps and that, but could we really have-"

"No. Maybe. No."

Sam's voice softened. "Well, something's going on out there. And you pulled that knife off the wreck."

"It wasn't even on the wreck. There's no stupid curse." Her ire rose. "This isn't my fault," she said.

"Maybe you set loose some evil spirit and now Emerson is dead. We were almost dead too, if you remember?"

"Evil spirit? Listen to yourself. Divers take trinkets off the bottom all the time. Do you really believe in some old wives' tale?"

"I don't know what to believe. I know what happened to us."

Heather made herself breathe before speaking. Sam was starting to sound like a lunatic conspiracy theorist. She didn't like being pushed to believe in anything, but something, obviously, wasn't right. "I'm sure there's some logical explanation. Listen, I don't want to talk about it right now. Maybe they'll have figured it out tomorrow. Let's talk about it then. Okay?"

They agreed to meet the following morning, after getting a much-needed night's sleep.

Sam had seemed like a reasonable man. Why was he letting this supernatural crap take root?

She turned and saw the black TV screen staring at her, poking, prodding, challenging her to widen her concept of reality as if it knew something she didn't. There wasn't any such thing as a curse.

Was there?

CHAPTER SIX

Sam inched open his eyes, letting the morning light in little by little. He was so glad it was Saturday, another day he did not have to work at the auto shop. What a lousy night. His sleep had been restless, if in fact he'd actually slept. The dark hours were filled with weird images and visions of ship-wrecks, knives, storms, stabbings, and a menacing, foul presence that stalked him in his dreams. He was glad it was over.

He looked over at the clock. 8:03 A.M. Good. He'd have plenty of time to shower and eat before going over to Heather's. He smiled to himself, realizing that he wanted to look his best when he saw her again.

After making himself presentable, he ate a breakfast sandwich, filled a travel mug with coffee and jumped into his truck.

It took him a grand total of five and a half minutes to get to Heather's house. Another benefit of small-town living. He pulled into the driveway and looked at the neatly-kept flower beds and the manicured lawn. Everything looked pleasant except the storm door that hung at a crooked angle, propped open with a stick to allow access to the front door. Easily fixed, yet it dangled, inoperable.

He hoped he wasn't too early.

Sam approached the front door on quiet feet, feeling that the house was at rest, hesitant to disturb its occupant. He didn't really know her. Maybe Heather was the type to bury her fears and drown her sorrows about her lost boat with wine or booze. He hoped she wasn't nursing a hangover. She had said to meet her here at 9:00, and 9:00 it was. He rapped-

The door opened.

"Morning," Heather said.

"Morning," Sam answered. She was dressed and manicured as if ready for a day at the office. Somehow, she looked better than she had in her diving suit.

She guided him into her small, historical two-story home, common in this old mining community. They sat opposite each other at her antique kitchen table. Sam noticed the rich wood framing around the doorways and the grainy crown molding. And the incessant drip from the kitchen sink.

"I can't believe Emerson's dead," Sam said.

"Yeah. I worked with his wife, Susan. Poor woman."

They stared at each other in silence, both

knowing why they were there, yet afraid to broach the subject directly. Finally, Sam said, "What the hell is going on?"

Heather shook her head. "I don't know."

"I think something tried to kill us yesterday, but it killed Emerson instead."

"I can't believe that," Heather said.

"Can't or won't?"

Heather sat in silence, lips pursed. Finally, "During our whole ordeal, did you ever feel cold?"

Sam scoured his memory. "No," he admitted.

"Right. And Emerson froze to death. I think we should worry about what happened to us first. We explain that it'll be a lot easier to see if Emerson's death is related or not."

"Emerson died where we almost died. Of course they're related. How can you not see that?"

Heather rubbed her forehead. "That may be. But whatever killed Emerson didn't kill us."

"It tried to," Sam said.

"What? What tried to kill us?" Heather was getting louder. "Nature? Or the boogeyman?"

It was Sam's turn to caress his head. He knew he was letting his imagination run away. But there was a connection here.

Sam bobbed his head. "Fine."

It didn't take long for them to propose and summarily dispel every rational explanation they could think of. They sat, staring at each other.

The young teacher frowned. Even her frown didn't diminish her simple beauty. "You said you thought the wave looked like the wake of some huge, submerged fish."

"A sea monster?" He creased his brow and gave a slight shake of his head. "I don't know. Thing would have to be enormous."

"What about some sort of submarine?"

"Maybe. But we would have seen it." Sam shook his head.

They returned to silence.

"What about the boiling water?" he said.

"I guess the wreck shifted and let loose some trapped air," she said.

Sam nodded in agreement. He moved his gaze around the house, his focus settling on a picture of a very young Heather. The photo reminded him of Maggie... He banished the thought and refocused his attention.

Heather shrugged. "Nothing makes sense." She folded her hands on the table. "I can't believe we seriously considered a sea monster."

"I may not be so well educated," Sam said. "But I believe I've heard it said, 'if it can't be explained by the ordinary, perhaps it's extraordinary.'"

Heather flopped against the back of her chair. "Are you talking about the curse?"

He nodded.

"Curses are superstition. They're just what people tag onto something they can't explain. Which explains nothing."

Sam dropped his gaze. He was frustrated and angry. And a little frightened, though he didn't want to admit it. He felt completely helpless. Glancing up, he saw Heather's eyes darting around, chasing a thought through her mind.

"Um," Heather said, sitting forward. "One of my old professors lives over in Hancock. He knew a lot about ancient curses and what not. We could talk to him. If nothing else, maybe he has some ideas."

So now she was entertaining the possibility of the supernatural too. "Let's go," Sam said.

During the brief ride to the home of Professor Grant Pekkonen, Heather fired a barrage of explanations she expected the professor would present. Each of them was based on coincidence, natural occurrences, imagination and misinterpretations that routinely gave rise to declarations of curses wreaking havoc in the normal world. She wanted to prepare Sam to hear that curses were just lore, legends, bullshit made up to explain what people couldn't. She'd heard the professor debunk several ancient curses, mostly because modern science could now explain things. He enjoyed students bringing in challenges like that. She hoped he still did.

She also explained to Sam that he would undoubtedly be offered candy corn. More likely, it would be forced upon him. It was a vice that Professor Pekkonen shared with great enthusiasm.

A long channel separated Hancock and the Keweenaw peninsula from the rest of Michigan's Upper Peninsula. Both the west and east ends of the channel opened onto Lake Superior. As usual, there were no big boats or ships traversing the tight channel. The world's heaviest lift bridge was passable to traffic, allowing them to zip from Houghton directly over to Hancock, putting them on the equivalent of a massive island.

They pulled into the driveway of a mid-sized Victorian home that appeared to be on the back side of its heyday. The house itself was an image of vintage coloring, yellow with forest green trim and door, but spots of cracking paint were starting to appear on the more exposed surfaces. The yard was slowly being retaken by the wilder, natural vegetation, though vibrant blossoms were scattered through flower beds, defiant, despite the choking greenery that curled around their stems.

Heather and Sam climbed out of the car, eager to engage Professor Pekkonen and hear what he had to say about the strange events of the last day. As an afterthought, Heather reached into the backseat and grabbed the knife she'd retrieved from the site of the Hawthorne's wreck and stuffed it into her sizable purse.

At the front door, Heather poked the doorbell and the two stood silent, like two kids nervously setting out on their first door-to-door sales pitch.

Nothing.

Finally, the door labored open and a smallish, white-haired man peered out at them with a tired smile. His face lit up.

"Oh! Ms. Case. How nice to see you. It's been too long."

He drew the door wider, motioning them in. When they'd assembled in the foyer the smiling old man grabbed Heather's shoulders and kissed her cheek. The light in his eyes dimmed when he looked at Sam, still maintaining his smile.

"And who is this?"

Heather introduced Sam and the two shook hands.

He ushered them into the sitting room where a television was tuned to the local station and gestured for them to make themselves comfortable. He ducked into the kitchen and returned with a bowl.

"Candy corn?" he asked.

Sam smiled. "I'm trying to quit."

"It's the Autumn Mix."

"Dammit. Okay," Sam said. He grabbed a handful.

Heather dug in and as the professor sat down, she glanced at Sam. "We were interested in getting your professional opinion on something." She popped some candy into her mouth.

The older man leaned back in his chair, eyes sparkling. "You want my impression of a novel?" A grin creased his lips.

"Well, no," Heather answered. "History. I recall you saying that you were interested in curses."

The professor tilted his head, eyebrows raised, but he nodded.

"Sam and I were talking about some strangebatterd"

"The Hawthorne Blow," the professor chuckled. "Is that what you're talking about?"

Heather nodded.

"One man freezing to death on Lake Superior in the middle of summer is hardly indicative of a curse."

Sam nodded. "Right, but there's more than that."

The professor frowned at Sam. "How so?"

"We were on the lake yesterday and something weird happened," Sam said.

The professor leaned forward, elbows on his knees and hands folded. "Weird?"

Sam recounted the previous day's events up until they reached Heather's boat. "That's when the wave hit us," Sam said.

"Wave?"

"A huge wave," Sam said. "Had to be thirty feet high. It sank Heather's boat."

"Did a storm blow in?" the professor asked.

"No." Heather said. "And the wave came from the direction of shore."

"Near the wreck?" the professor asked. His brow creased and a powerful frown distorted his mouth.

"There's a logical explanation for all of this stuff. Right?" Heather asked.

The professor raised his shoulders, holding his palms up. "Usually." He took a deep breath. "There have been curses throughout history that are unexplained."

Sam and Heather exchanged concerned looks.

Professor Pekkonen continued. "In June 1941, Stalin order Russian anthropologists to find and exhume the body of a fourteenth century warlord named Tamerlane in Uzbekistan. The local Muslim clerics were wholly against it and warned that disaster would befall them three days later. Tamerlane's body was exhumed and three days later Nazi Germany launched their invasion of Russia."

"Germany was invading everybody in those days," Sam said through a frown.

"Yes. But Stalin eventually ordered the body to be buried again, with full Muslim rites. Soon after that, Russia defeated Germany in the Battle of Stalingrad. That victory put Russia on the offensive."

Sam and Heather sat silent, the professor's words leaving tracks in their brains.

"As in that example, the only unexplained curses I know of were all set off by defacing or stealing from a site of historical or religious significance. Whether the resulting disasters were supernatural or not still cannot be explained. What did you do on the wreck? Did you disturb it or deface it in any way?"

Sam nudged Heather with his elbow, motioning to her handbag with his face.

Heather pursed her lips. "I found this," she said, producing the old knife. "It wasn't on the wreck," she said, glaring at Sam before continuing, "just near it."

The professor reached out with both hands to take the dagger and turned it over as he examined it.

"This looks to be about the right age to have come from the Hawthorne," he said. "But I'm no expert on antiquities." His face became grave and he handed the knife back to Heather. "I'm loath to label anything as a curse. But-" He stopped and picked up the TV remote control and raised the volume. There was a breaking news story; another boat had been found with two people frozen to death. This one was in Keweenaw Bay, much closer to Houghton than the first.

Professor Pekkonen inclined his head towards the dagger in Heather's hands. "Looks like something wants that knife back."

CHAPTER SEVEN

The short drive back to Heather's was a quiet one. Sam wasn't sure what to make of the professor's comment and Heather pouted in silence. She certainly wasn't buying into talk about a curse. When he dropped her off, she said little other than that she would talk to him later.

Though he had always enjoyed adventure stories about magic and good versus evil, Sam had never considered that a curse could be real. And deadly. The events lately had him very concerned about the boogeyman.

When Sam arrived back at his house, he noticed Lily sitting on her front porch with her face resting in her hands, looking distraught. He sighed to himself and parked his truck in the driveway and prepared to go talk to her. Again? What he really wanted to do was have a beer and not think. But he knew he was on Lily's short list of friends.

He walked across the street and sat down next to her after she made room for him.

"How's it going?" he asked.

"Did you see the news?"

Sam nodded.

"How does someone freeze to death in the middle of summer? Turned to ice?" Her voice had that dismayed tone Sam typically heard from teenage girls second-guessing another girl's fashion choices.

"Beats me," he answered. "Must be some sort of weird weather phenomenon." He hoped he sounded more convincing than he felt.

Lily turned to face him. "What if my vision has something to do with what happened?"

Sam wrinkled his eyebrows. "I doubt that. Wasn't your vision about me and Jake getting stabbed or something?"

Her lips pursed and she gave a slight nod.

"And we were older than we are now?"

Again, she nodded. "But it looked like you were on a boat and these guys are dying out in their boats."

"But not getting stabbed."

"Yeah, but I didn't see *them* dying. I saw you and Jake. Death is death," she said, the volume of her voice rising. "I don't know how these fucking visions work! Sometimes I see exactly what is going to happen. Usually not."

Sam stared at his feet. He couldn't understand what she was going through, but he wanted to hear her out. At the same time, he didn't think her vision had anything to do with the men freezing to death out on the lake. Yes, death was death. But freezing seemed a far cry from stabbing. "I'm sorry, Lily. I have no idea how your visions work either. But I really doubt you saw something that had to do with what happened to those guys." He saw her gazing at the ground, a lost look in her eyes. "I don't think there is anything you could have done to prevent that."

"Then why am I having these visions?"

Sam thought about it. "Maybe so you could warn me and Jake. Which you have," he added. "If we're ever out on a boat, or just together sometime, I'll know to be careful."

She wiped a tear that slid quietly down her cheek and bobbed her head. Her brow creased and she inclined her head. "Were any of the men that died named Melville?"

"No. I knew Emerson."

Lily blanched. "I'm sorry."

Sam gave her a weak, but reassuring smile. "I don't recall the names of the other guys, but neither was Melville. Why do you ask?"

"I remember something in my vision and that name."

Sam pulled out his cell phone and searched the name 'Melville'. After a few minutes of checking different towns nearby for the name he shook his head. "Doesn't look like there's anyone around town with that name. At least not listed. What are you thinking?"

"Melville has some significance. I just don't know what. Just like I don't know where my vision takes place, or why you and Jake are older, or who the other guy is." Fresh tears started to roll down her cheeks. "Why do I have these stupid things anyway?"

Sam reached over and put his hand on hers. Instantly her head snapped up and her mouth sprang wide, her eyes darted in crazy patterns before finally rolling back and closing.

"No! No," she screamed. Her body went limp and Sam had to catch her before she fell face-first onto the sidewalk.

The front door of Lily's house flew open and her father, Tim, came out, his body ready for a fight. Fierce eyes locked on Sam.

"I think she's having a vision," Sam said. He kept his eyes on Tim, hoping he wasn't about to get hit.

Tim quickly reached for his teenage daughter. "What happened? Did you touch her?"

"Yeah. I just patted her hand and-"

"Don't touch her, Sam," Tim said.

"I'm sorry. I-"

"You should go," he said. He scooped Lily into his arms as if she weighed no more than a sack of flour and carried her into the house as her body shuddered and twitched.

Sam walked back towards his house. Twice he glanced back, concerned that he had triggered one of Lily's episodes. How did that happen? He found himself contemplating the events of the past day and a half. The roiling water by the sunken ship, the massive wave that destroyed Heather's boat, Emerson freezing to death near the wreck, two other men freezing to death closer to town, and Lily having visions. Visions about him.

And the only man he'd ever met who claimed to know anything about real curses had said just this morning that there well may be a curse.

A wave had nearly drowned him yesterday and Lily was having visions of him getting stabbed to death.

If there really was a curse, it seemed that Sam was dead in its sights.

CHAPTER EIGHT

Jeff Randall drew in the fresh lake air as he strolled down the boardwalk that ran along Houghton's canal. The channel cut through the Keweenaw peninsula, providing access to Portage Lake for big ore carriers that wanted to shelter from storms. The evening air was cooling, but still held plenty of warmth. This far north meant that though it was past ten o'clock in the evening, there was still enough daylight to see for miles.

Randall had sailing in his blood. He was descended from a long line of mariners dating back to the late 1800s. His family had started out on ocean-going vessels but had migrated to working on the Great Lakes, a life some might say was less perilous. In 1886, when Houghton and Hancock were thriving mining towns, the region was struck by a diphtheria epidemic. One of his ancestors was a crew member on the ship that carried antitoxin to treat the outbreak. The ship hit a terrible November storm as it raced westward on Lake Superior, struggling to make it to the shelter of the Houghton canal. Luckily, the crew and captain performed magnificently, bringing the ship to dock and delivering the medicine. The day after their arrival, one third of the crew quit or retired, citing the extreme stress they had endured in making that trip.

Randall smiled to himself as he imagined the courage of all the men as the steam ship crashed through the unforgiving swells of the big lake.

Now retired, Randall had once piloted the huge ore carriers that transported iron ore from Michigan's upper peninsula down to Cleveland. He always enjoyed seeing the big, glamorous sailing vessels that would cruise the lakes on occasion. Though no longer a choice for cargo, the pleasure boats were plentiful enough to bring back a fanciful nostalgia to any Great Lakes mariner. When he saw the three-master at the dock, he knew he had to see it up close.

The sun, well below the horizon, was losing its influence quickly. Colors blended into simple shades of gray. And so it was that the big vessel took on a drab, smoky appearance, losing the flash she must have displayed in full daylight. Nonetheless, Randall was impressed both by her size and the authentic nature of her construction. The deck was nearly five feet above the dock. Impressive for a sailing boat. A gangplank extended down to the dock as the ship rested on tranquil waters.

"Ahoy," Randall shouted. No one answered

and he couldn't see lights anywhere on board.

"Hello! Is anyone aboard?" He stopped at the base of the gangplank and waited. He looked up and down the boardwalk, hoping he might see someone approaching. He thought he heard some clunking from on board but saw no one.

A cool breeze picked up, coming off the channel. Not enough to disturb the water, but enough to make Randall shiver once. Involuntarily, his eyes were drawn to the big main mast that towered above the center of the ship. It dwarfed the fore mast and mizzen mast, though they were both bigger than any he'd seen up close. Like the trunks of powerful redwoods, they were all bigger than any he'd ever see again. He was mesmerized by the very tip of the mast, so impossibly distant. It was definitely a place he would not want to find himself.

The sky above darkened, quickly now that the sun was fully set. Randall didn't want to go onto the ship uninvited. He gave another shout, "Anyone here?"

Nothing.

He was about to head home when he caught a sound coming from the stern on his right. A figure emerged from below deck, slowly, with steps like that of an old man in no hurry. The figure waved for Randall to come aboard.

"Ahoy, there," Randall said. "Are you the

captain of this beau-" The words caught in his throat when the man faced him. Even from twenty feet away in fading light, it was clear his eyes were void of empathy, black and cruel. Randall was struck dumb by the simmering evil that radiated from the man, his stare now taking on a blue hue.

Randall backed away.

The man pointed a pale, withered finger in Randall's direction.

Too late, Randall realized his mistake.

His corpse tumbled down the gangplank with a clunk, the impact sending tiny shards of ice into the gray air as they broke from his frozen sarcophagus and landed on the boardwalk.

CHAPTER NINE

Sunday. Hangover. Not a bad one, but Sam didn't usually imbibe enough to feel it the next morning. After Lily's episode last evening, he'd spent a little too much time feeling a little too melancholy and sipping a little too much rum and Coke.

A nice, hot shower proved to be medicine enough for his lagging spirits. No doubt an ibuprofen and coffee would take care of the slight throbbing in his head.

As he waited for the coffee to brew, he flipped on the radio. Another body was found frozen to death. This one on the canal boardwalk. Jeff Randall. Sam didn't know him, but it didn't really matter.

He was still processing the news when the phone rang.

It was Heather. "Did you hear?"

"Yeah."

"How the hell are they *freezing* to death?"

Sam thought for a minute. "I dunno. Liquid nitrogen?"

"Hmmm. One report said the body was encased in a block of ice. Liquid nitrogen would freeze them so solid they'd shatter."

"I wasn't being serious," Sam said. "I'm out of ideas."

"Oh." He heard her wheeze out a breath. "Can you come over?" Heather asked.

He sighed. "I have to get some coffee in me, then I'll be over."

"Sam! Sam!" It was Lily. She was running across the street.

He put on his best smile. "Hey Lily. How are you feeling?"

"It was you, and an older Jake again. But this time Jake was dead and his body was sliding around in water on the deck of a boat. It was snowing, and storming. There was a big mast and you and this other guy were fighting. The other guy had a knife."

Sam held up his hands. "Hold on. Slow down," he said. "Who had a knife?"

She shrugged. "I didn't recognize him. Anyway, during the fight the guy stabs you over and over. Until you die."

Sam stared at the girl in hushed silence. Not exactly what he wanted to hear. At all. Her crazy stories were starting to get inside his head. She saw him being murdered? He couldn't deal with this right now.

He walked to his truck and opened the door before stopping. "Tell you what. I won't go on any sail boats, especially in a storm. Okay?"

Lily sighed and she cast her face down. Half-heartedly she asked, "Promise?"

"I promise," Sam said. Lily was still gazing at the ground. *Dammit, she's not buying it.* He stared at the young woman for a minute. What if her visions had something to do with what was happening with the other deaths? "Did you ever have Heather Case for a teacher?"

The young woman perked up. "Ms. Case? Yeah. Last year. She was awesome."

"I'm heading over to her house now. Maybe she can help us figure out your visions. You want to come along?" Heather might have some insights that he was missing.

"Okay."

"Better check with your folks. They may not be really happy after what happened yesterday."

Lily ran into the house and came out a few minutes later.

"Yeah, I can go. Just don't, you know, touch me."

Sam laughed and shook his head. "No argument from me."

Heather's face scrunched up as she looked at

Lily. She shifted her attention to Sam, who sat next to her.

"That story isn't helping me to stick to any logical, scientific reason for what's going on."

"I'm sorry," Lily said.

Heather reached across the kitchen table and patted her hand, eliciting a gasp from Sam.

"Did Sam tell you what happened to us?"

Sam's golden eyes snapped wide. He shook his head and tried to wave Heather off, but it was too late.

"No. What happened?"

Heather ran down the events starting with his catching her on his fishing lure to the wave nearly drowning both of them. Lily turned a horrified look on Sam.

"Why didn't you tell me?"

"I didn't think it was related."

Lily gave a slight nod and turned back to Heather, throwing a sideways glance back at Sam, her face now analytical and stoic. "You really think my visions might have something to do with what's going on?"

Heather shrugged. "Could be. I'd like Dr. Pekkonen's thoughts, though."

Lily pressed against the back of her chair and shook her head. "No. I'm not going to a doctor."

Sam smiled at Lily. "Not that kind of doctor. He's a retired professor."

She eyed him suspiciously, squinting. Finally, she said, "I guess that'd be okay.

When Grant Pekkonen answered the door, his face was drawn and pale. "You heard," he stated. "Please, come in." He gave a questioning look at Lily but said nothing.

All four walked into the living room, silence enveloping them. The television and radio were off and closed windows shut out any noise from the occasional passing car. With no flow of air, the place smelled musty and old, forgotten. When everyone was seated, the professor sat back in his cushy, Victorian chair and surveyed his visitors.

"Who's this?" the professor asked. He flashed a tired but warm smile at Lily.

"Lily Swanson," she answered. She reached her hand out and the professor grasped it warmly with both his, like a grandfather welcoming one of his grand-children's friends.

"You may want to hear what she has to say," Heather provided.

The professor nodded and huffed out a laugh. "First, I have to tell you something."

Sam and Heather locked eyes in a brief sideways glance. "What?" Sam said.

"The fourth body," the professor said. "The Curse of the Hawthorne."

Lily let out a squeak. "Curse?"

The old professor nodded.

Sam sighed. "There must be some other explanation." Though in his head, he'd already come to that conclusion.

"Why would there even be a Hawthorne curse?" Heather asked.

The professor met eyes with each of his guests, one by one, and breathed deeply. "So none of you have heard the story?" At their blank stares he continued. "I guess that doesn't surprise me much. Seems none of you know anything anymore that isn't published on the Internet. True or false. The art of oral history is almost dead."

"You mean urban legends?" Lily asked.

The professor's face hardened and he fixed Lily with a stare. "No, Lily. Not urban legend. Facts. Truth passed down from generation to generation. The way it has been done for thousands of years, until that damned Internet came along." He leaned forward in his chair, elbows on knees, hands folded in front. Once they were all paying rapt attention, he began.

"In fall of 1886 a diphtheria outbreak occurred here in the Keweenaw Peninsula. People started dying before they realized what was happening. They got word downstate to Detroit and a ship, the Melville, was returning to Houghton and volunteered to bring a load of antitoxin. A lot of the sailors had family that were at risk, so they were eager to make the trip. Sailing in November meant a risky journey. Unfortunately, they were caught in an early winter storm, later named the 'Hawthorne Blow', and did everything they could do to make it to Houghton. Ultimately they made it and they delivered the medicine."

"So what's this 'Curse of the Hawthorne'?" Sam asked.

The professor's head dropped and he took a deep breath. "That is what very few people know the truth about. They've heard the phrase but not the story behind it. During the final leg across Superior, the Melville happened upon the Hawthorne. She had somehow taken on water in the storm and sunk. But because she was a three-master, and the water was relatively shallow, the main mast stuck up out of the water. The Melville sailed closed enough to it to see that one survivor clung to the mast, waving, needing to be saved. As much as it pained him to do it, the captain gave the command to sail on, not wanting to risk his ship and cargo for one soul. After the storm, the poor sailor from the Hawthorne, Fitch Krause, was found in three inches of ice, frozen to the mast.

Dead. About a third of the crew of the Melville resigned the next day. Some because they had begged the captain to rescue the man, some because of the guilt they felt for supporting the captain's decision. And that is where the curse is said to have originated: from the sailors leaving one of their own to die."

"That sounds like a well thought-up tale, professor. What makes you so sure it's even real?" Heather asked.

The professor's lips pinched into a frown. "Because the captain was my great-great-grandfathcr. And I have his journal. The journal in which he describes the agony of having to leave that man to die."

The room thrummed with an uneasy silence. Everyone taking in the gravity of what the professor had laid out.

"So that's why these guys are being frozen to death? You think it's some kind of ghost or spirit or something taking revenge for being left on that mast?" Sam asked.

Heather frowned. "I don't know."

"As far as curses go, that is the best explanation," the professor added. "Especially if you consider the four men killed."

"What about them?" Sam asked.

The professor paused as he caught Sam's eye. "All four of them were descendants of sailors from the Melville."

Sam caught his breath.

"Are any of you descended from the crew of the Melville?" the professor asked.

Heather and Lily shook their heads.

"I'm actually a descendant of someone who died on the Hawthorne," Sam answered. "I thought it was just an unfortunate shipwreck."

The professor's eyes narrowed. "Now that's interesting."

Heather turned to Lily. "I think you better tell him what you saw."

Lily turned this way and that, restless in her chair. Her eyebrows crumpled on her forehead and she gave a slight shake of her head. Not in denial, but in frustration or confusion. Sam hated seeing her like this; it reminded him of his little sister, Maggie, before she had overdosed. Anxious, twitchy and perpetually disoriented. He couldn't go through something like that again.

"Lily, what's wrong?" he asked, more sternly than he wanted.

She quit wiggling and looked at the professor. "The ship was the Melville? I saw that name in my vision."

Professor Pekkonen turned to Heather.

"Vision?"

"Go ahead," Heather said to Lily.

Lily squirmed some more before finally locking her feet around the legs of her chair. Finally, she told the professor everything.

The professor sat back, rubbing his chin, eyes distant. "Was there anything else?"

Lily started as though she'd just remembered where she'd left her keys. "Oh, right! I saw the name Melville, in gold lettering. Like the name of the boat you were talking about."

Sam was thrown off by the revelation of seeing the ship's name. That didn't make sense. Unless there was a new ship coming to town in the next couple of days with that same name. He could see Heather and the professor working it around in their heads too.

"That is odd," the professor said. "Unless it is a way of verifying that the curse is related to the Melville. But I honestly don't understand the significance of the knife fight."

"I think it's something that is going to happen," Lily said.

"But I only know Jake from the hardware store. Why would we ever be on a boat together and get into a situation where someone could stab us?" Sam said.

"Yeah. Something is missing," Heather added. "Are you sure there wasn't anything else in your vision?"

"I told you everything," Lily said, shrugging.

"Maybe she saw something historical? Though, how it relates to what is happening now, I don't know," the professor said. After a few moments he asked, "When did you start having these visions?"

Lily thought for a moment. "Two days ago, I think. Yeah. Friday. The first one came when I was at the hardware store."

The professor looked at Sam and Heather. "Isn't that the day you two had your run-in with the rogue wave?"

Sam nodded.

"What time did that happen?" the professor asked.

"I don't really know what time," Heather said. "Must have been about three, three-thirty?"

"And what time did you go to the hardware store?" he asked Lily.

"Sometime in the afternoon. Closer to four, probably."

"So they could be related," the professor stated. "I'm not sure how. But at this point I'm not thinking it's a coincidence." He lifted his chin and leaned back, staring through the ceiling. "You found a knife near the wreck?"

Realization washed over Heather's face. "Yeah."

"You brought the knife up, and soon thereafter, you are nearly killed, four men are frozen to death in the middle of summer, and this young lady starts having visions." He scanned his captive audience.

"When you put it like that, it does sound like a curse," Heather said.

"Maybe you should take the knife back out there and throw it in the lake," Lily said to Heather.

"I'm willing to give it a shot," Heather said.

"We can take my boat," Sam said.

But Professor Pekkonen was shaking his head. "I think it's too late for that."

"Why?" Heather asked.

"The spirit has been disturbed. It's on the hunt for revenge. And it's taking it. It's killing every relation of any sailor that was onboard the Melville. Who do you think it really wants?"

"The captain," Lily blurted. Then she shriveled in on herself, realizing what she'd said.

The professor smiled gently at Lily. "Yes. He wants the one man who made the decision to leave him out there to freeze to death."

Sam regarded the professor without saying a word, slowly starting to shake his head. "Listen. I doubt your death will make anything stop."

The professor pursed his lips. "I didn't say anything about dying. Maybe there's some way I can ask for forgiveness on behalf of the whole crew. At least that's my plan."

"What if it just kills you?" Heather asked.

The professor shrugged. "I just go a little early then." His weak smile faded away as he looked at the picture of his deceased wife on the shelf. "I'm almost dead anyway."

CHAPTER TEN

Sam, Heather and Lily stared at the professor, speechless. After several moments of awkward silence, Sam found his voice.

"You're dying?"

"Hmm," the professor replied. "Lymphoma."

More silence.

"I'm sorry," Heather said.

"Everyone has to go. My wife is gone. No kids. And if I can help stop whatever this power is from killing anyone else, no regrets."

"You shouldn't just sacrifice yourself," Lily said. "All of this started when Heather brought up that knife. Right? We need to put the knife back."

The professor regarded the girl, echoes of the old teacher playing on his features.

"What makes you think that will do it?" the professor asked. His face glowed as he grasped his chin in one hand, waiting for her answer.

Lily leaned forward. "If we throw it back into the lake, it won't be around to be used on Sam and Jake, like in my visions."

"She's got a point," Sam said.

Professor Pekkonen shook his head. "If it

were that simple, Heather would most likely have been the sole target. Perhaps you too, Sam. But four descendants have been killed. That is deliberate. It's working its way up the chain of command. The sooner it gets to me, the sooner it ends."

"But you're talking about possibly going to your death," Sam said.

"Not necessarily," the professor countered. He didn't believe his own words, but in order to get around an argument, he had to throw them a bone. "Maybe there is some way for me to make amends, if I can talk to this thing."

"He's got a point, Sam," Heather said. "I don't like it, but it seems like the best chance."

Lily stomped her feet. "Then why did it try to kill both of you? You said neither of you are descendants. Explain that." She crossed her arms, mouth tightly closed.

"Yeah," Sam agreed. "The only reason I can think of for it trying to kill us is because we had the knife." Sam thought for a moment. "You realize we don't even really know what we are dealing with?"

"I thought it was a curse," Lily said.

"Sam is right," the professor said. "We don't know what form this curse takes. I'm assuming it is some spirit or form that can be seen and addressed. But we don't know."

"The news reports said something about a fog

and a ghost ship during the first attack." Heather said. "If that's true, we should be able to see the ship."

"So what?" Lily said. "Let's just take the knife and throw it back on the wreck. We don't need to see it to do that."

"I don't think that is going to help," the professor reiterated. "I need to do something, as the de facto captain, I'm the one who needs to fix this. I have to give peace to this tortured soul."

Lily slammed her fists on her thighs. "Bullshit! We need to get rid of the knife," she screamed. She turned watery eyes on Sam.

Sam fixed his eyes on her, knowing she believed if the knife was still here, he was going to die. He wasn't convinced that was the case, but he did share her belief that the knife's absence from the wreck was what was causing this thing to go around killing. After all, everything started happening when Heather brought that thing out of the lake. It wouldn't take long: get down to his boat, jump in and motor out to the wreck, throw the antique dagger back in. At most an hour and a half.

"What if the curse is limited by where the knife is? Why keep it here?" Sam said. "Doesn't cost us anything to throw it back."

"Just time," Heather said. "But I'm not particularly anxious to go back out in a boat. Are you?" She stared at Sam.

Sam puffed out his cheeks as he exhaled, deflating. "Not really. But we know how to do that. How could we get the professor in a position to 'apologize', or whatever the hell he wants to do? We don't know that there is even anything to apologize to."

"We'll figure it out," Heather said.

Everyone sat stewing, rolling over plans and possibilities in their minds. How do you track down something that may not be visible? How do you reason with something that may simply kill you before you know it's even there? What if the apology or reasoning fails?

"How about this," Sam said. "We get rid of the knife first. If that doesn't seem to work, then we'll try your way." Two weak nods from Heather and the professor and an enthusiastic nod from Lily. "Okay. You got the knife?" he asked Heather.

"It's at home," she answered.

Lily jumped up and went to the door, eager to get rid of the terrifying instrument of death from her visions.

"Let's go get it and get this done," Sam said.

"Uh," Lily interjected, staring out the door at a world that had gone darker than any storm Sam had experienced. A wet, foggy mist shrouded the driveway, obscuring the road completely and cold air rolled in through the open door like the frigid waters of the big lake surging into a warm bay. Her lower lip trembling, she said, "We might be too late."

CHAPTER ELEVEN

Jake Henderson was at the beach, waiting for his two football buddies to show up. They were going to spend the day hanging out, cooling off in the water, and scoping for chicks. He wasn't sure the last part made any sense, as the town was small enough that they knew everyone their age in both Hancock and Houghton. At least the girls. But once in a while there would be a family in from out of town, enjoying the upper peninsula summer, and they'd have a teenage girl who'd be like discovering a new species of flower among the roses you knew so well. And honestly, Jake kind of liked Silly Lily. He'd never call her that, didn't even want to think of her that way. But the name was used so often by other kids, it was hard not to slip into the habit yourself.

He wondered about the other day, when she was in the hardware store. There were stories of her flipping out, claiming to have visions. But to him it looked like some sort of weird seizure. When she regained control, she didn't say anything about having a 'vision'. And she had wet herself, something he wouldn't mention to anyone. Perhaps part of his attraction to her was because she was an outcast. Jake felt somewhat protective of her. He didn't appreciate anyone being subjected to ridicule and cruelty. A little joke now and then, in good humor, was okay. But most of the kids made a hobby of poking fun at her.

Looking down at his bare chest, arms and thighs, Jake realized that all of the working out he was doing for football was starting to show. And other kids had noticed too. He was getting bigger and stronger. And scarier. At that moment he decided to make use of that image and stand up for Lily. He'd start today, by mentioning to his friends that she'd come into the store and she'd seemed really nice.

Tyler and Dan came cruising into the parking lot on their bikes, towels draped around their necks. They skidded up to Jake then stuck their rides in the bicycle rack.

"Any new girls?" Dan asked.

"Nothin'," Jake answered.

"One'll turn up," Tyler said. "It's the middle of summer. They always turn up."

They started walking down to the sandy beach, the biggest, Jake, flanked by the other two.

"Lily came into the store Friday," he said.

"Silly Lily?" Dan asked.

Jake scowled. "Don't call her that."

"Why not? She's weird."

"She's not weird. I think she just has a medical problem. She had a seizure when she was there."

"Ooooh. Did she say she had a vision?" Dan said.

Tyler reached over and smacked Dan on the chest, frowning. Then he looked at Jake. "What do you mean?" he asked.

Jake shrugged. "A seizure. You know. Her body kind of locked up and she fell. She looked really scared when she came out of it. I felt bad for her."

"I have a cousin that has seizures," Tyler said.

Jake nodded, sensing support from one of his friends. "Yeah. I don't think we should make fun of her. What if she was your sister?"

"She's not," Dan said. "She's Silly Lily."

Jake punched Dan in the arm, hard. Dan immediately started rubbing the spot where the bruise would eventually grow. "I'm serious. Knock it off."

"Fair enough," Tyler said, putting an extra two feet between him and Jake.

"Fine," Dan said. "Just 'Lily'."

Jake smiled to himself. He knew Tyler was a little softer than Dan, but Dan wasn't a complete tool. Sometimes he just needed a push.

A cold breeze washed over his feet as they

wandered around on the small beach. It was a very cold breeze, from off the channel. He turned toward the water and saw a massive gray cloud that extended well into the sky sliding up the channel from the east, pushing a wall of fog in front of it. He'd never seen anything quite like it.

Everyone was staring at it. No one was smiling.

"What's that?" he asked, gesturing with his chin.

The boys shook their heads. "Weird." Dan said.

Faster than he would have thought possible, the fog and clouds enveloped the beachgoers, bringing with it a cold that penetrated even his soul. The boys wasted no time in pulling on their T-shirts, wrapping their towels around hunched shoulders. Weather in the upper peninsula changed quickly, but this was like nothing they'd ever experienced.

And then the stories of the men who were found frozen to death leaped into Jake's consciousness, eliciting a growing feeling of panic. Was he about to freeze to death? Were all of the people here going to die with him?

He looked at his two friends. "Run!"

Jake was too young to die. He ran for his bike and threw his leg over it and laid into the pedals with all his might, Tyler and Dan close behind. Still watching the channel and the fog, something just to the east on the water caught his attention. A ship. Three masts in full, ragged, sail. Black and broken the ship looked, with shattered timbers forming its sides, pocked with huge holes that ran down below the water line. And at the most forward point of the bow stood a man. Or what passed as a man: white with a dark maw for his mouth, sailor's garb that hung tattered from his body, and icy blue eyes that, despite the hundreds of yards of distance, sought out Jake Henderson and locked onto him like an osprey's finding a young fish that swam too close to the surface.

The man raised his arm and his finger slowly extended outward from a closed fist, pointing directly at Jake.

"Come on," Jake yelled. With renewed vigor Jake pedaled off the beach through the parking lot and started up the long hill to his house, his friends close behind. That man, or whatever it was, had just pointed at him. He was sure of it. But why?

People ran to their vehicles, scooping up toddlers and young children in a desperate exodus. Cars smashed into one another as drivers sought to escape this foreboding ghost ship that glided along the channel's now black waters. Horns honked and people screamed and cried. He saw Dan break off and head down the street toward his own house. Soon, Tyler would do the same.

The commotion started to fade as Jake climbed steadily away from the beach, sounds falling off in the dense fog that now covered the entire channel. He tried to see across the water to Hancock, but his view was blocked by a massive gray cloud. Even the big lift-bridge was swallowed up by the mist.

Now his ears were filled with the sound of air rushing into his burning lungs. He had to slow down and catch his breath. He allowed himself to sit down on the seat of his mountain bike and dropped the gears down to a more powerful ratio. The bike slowed noticeably even as it progressed up the incline, but the fire in his legs started to subside.

Tyler broke off, heading for his home. "Call me when you get home," he shouted.

Jake waved acknowledgment.

What was going on? That horrible thing looked like an honest-to-God ghost ship. And the cold! It must be what was freezing guys to death in the middle of summer. But why? The image of the sailor pointing at him sent a different chill through him, knowing it had been a threat. Was it coming for him? Why would some unbelievable phantom want to threaten or hurt him?

Home was only a mile away. Jake's legs had regained their strength and he geared up for more speed, wanting like a little boy to be safe in his house where his parents could protect him. He wondered then if they could.

With only a couple more blocks to go, the air became frigid again. Not the kind of cold that would freeze anything, but akin to an early November breeze. In the middle of July, the chill was beyond unnatural. The young man's breath shone as white puffs of mist under his nose.

He could see his house now, a sanctuary beaconing him to its warmth and shelter. Speeding into the driveway he leapt from his bike, letting it fall wherever it chanced to land. He charged to the door. Pain lanced through his hand when he grabbed the icy knob and he hissed in shock. Ignoring the ache, he flung the door wide.

"Mom! Dad!"

No answer. They should be home. He called again with the same result. A dark feeling settled in his stomach, wringing the acid up into his throat.

He listened. Nothing.

A dank, stale smell filled his nostrils, bringing back memories of gutting a whitetail on a brutally cold November morning. Then, it was a scent associated with good times with his father, enjoying nature and the management of it. Now it was the stink of something dire and evil.

Like a hunter Jake stalked through the house, quickly covering the first floor, finding no one. Up the stairs he climbed, the floor of the hallway first coming into view, then the open door to his room, and finally the frosty and splintered door to his parents' room.

His heart thumped in a panicked rhythm, his breathing shallow and quick. A ringing sounded in his ears, throbbing in unison with his pulse. The coppery scent of blood assailed his nostrils. Moving with a haste born of concern he flew to the shattered doorway and looked inside.

Jake's parents were in a bloody embrace, his father sheltering his mother, both dead. A loving couple transformed into a macabre, mangled heap laying in a crimson pool, despair and horror eternally recorded on their faces. He was too stunned to cry; he could only stare.

Police. He had to call the police. His parents were dead. Pulling his cell phone out of his pocket he held it in front of his face. What was the police number? He didn't have it programmed in his contacts. How the hell are you supposed to call the police? Oh, right. Nine-one-one. Jake punched in the number and hit the call button. Nothing. Tears streamed down his cheeks. He looked at the phone.

No signal. He usually had four bars.

The police station was only five blocks away. He'd ride down there and tell them what happened. It would probably be safer there anyway.

Descending the stairs felt like he was lowering himself into a tub full of ice-water. Cold enveloped him as he descended, creeping from foot to head, covering more and more of his body with each step he walked down. He felt the pale blue eyes on him before he saw them. When he was still two steps from the bottom of the staircase, he saw it.

What had frightened him at a distance of three-hundred yards, terrified him as it stood in his front hall. The tattered remnants of a man waited a mere ten feet away. His skin was pasty, bloated and gnawed, hunks of flesh missing from various parts of his skeletal face. White scalp was exposed between patches of hair that hung in gnarled, moldy clumps. What was left of a thick wool coat and wool trousers mercifully covered most of the walking corpse's body. But nothing covered the menacing, blue eyes that shot forth pure hatred. There was nothing protecting Jake from those eyes.

"Wha...what do you want?" Jake asked.

The voice that answered was the sound of a pit of vipers. "You will be silent." The creature stared at him, quiet, unmoving.

Jake examined the supernatural killer in front

of him and a strange stillness filled his body. The fear seeped away even as he realized what he faced. Upstairs, his mother and father crouched together in a last futile act of unity. And this thing before him had committed the heinous act. Anger rushed to fill the void left by the fear.

"You killed my parents," Jake screamed. Then, with a blind rage true to his ancestry, Jake launched himself at the monster, reaching for its throat.

Jake was dead before he hit the ground.

CHAPTER TWELVE

Lily climbed into the bed of Sam's truck so the professor could take a place in the cab with Sam and Heather. Like an over-protective brother Sam told her to sit down and made her promise to hold on tight. He didn't plan on driving fast, but he wasn't going on a Sunday drive.

He flipped on the headlights as they pulled out of the professor's driveway, the thick gray fog limiting visibility to only fifty yards.

"This isn't natural," the professor said, looking around at the oppressive mist.

"You think it's the curse?" Heather asked him.

"Lily's right. We may be too late."

Sam stopped and turned right, straining to see if any traffic was coming. "Let's just get the damned knife and get it out to the wreck."

The professor looked at Sam from the corner of his eye.

"What if we run into whatever is causing this before we get to my house?" Heather asked. She looked at her old professor.

"Then we do things my way."

"Ah, shit," Sam said. "Fine. We run into it; you do your thing. But I'm still taking Lily to get that knife."

Sam steered the truck through a couple more turns and dodged some potholes before they were on US-41, heading for the bridge that would take them back over to Houghton. The sun was a dull white orb in the dark clouds, its brilliance and warmth choked by the strange fog. Sets of headlights approached and went flying past. Fast. Soon more of them appeared. And more. Each vehicle driving faster than was safe given the limited visibility.

Ahead, Sam saw a line of red taillights. He came to a halt behind the last vehicle.

People were getting out of their cars, confused and looking around. Sam, Heather and Professor Pekkonen joined them, Lily springing out of the back. The four walked forward to talk with the next driver when another car came zooming out of the mist and raced away. Sam could see a group of people standing around a delivery truck farther up in line. When their little group got closer, Sam could see there would be more questions than answers from the assemblage.

"What's going on?" the professor asked one of the other drivers.

"I guess the bridge lifted for a ship and the thing hit it in the fog. Now it's stuck and they can't lower it," the woman answered.

"Why is everyone flying past here?"

"Something else is happening down there," a man said. He was watching up the road, craning his neck this way and that, trying to see.

"Crap," the professor said. He turned to Sam and Heather. "We might be here a while."

"We don't have time for this," Lily said. "We have to get that knife back out to the wreck."

Another car raced by from the direction of the bridge, its driver heedless of the people milling around on the road.

A scream echoed up the street from ahead. Followed by shouts and more screams. Then people were running at them, in full flight, coming one or two at a time, faces twisted by dread. Sam, Heather and Lily all looked at the professor. The corners of his mouth edged up into what may have been a smile, but if it was, it was in poor humor.

"Looks like it's plan 'B'," the professor said.

They stood on the lower level of the bridge, where the old train tracks crossed. High above their heads, the two-tiered lift section was suspended, frozen in place by thick sheets of ice, not damaged by any freighter as they'd been told. Fifty yards of open water rippled between them and the other side of the bridge. To their left the fog thinned enough that the marina was clearly visible. Unfortunately. Sam could see several frozen bodies scattered along the piers. At the end of the largest pier a large, gray, three-masted schooner was moored, the water around it flat as glass. With the wind dead, moldy and stained sails hung lifeless from the yards. The ship appeared badly damaged, yet floated upright without a list, as though it had just been launched from dry-dock.

Near the water's edge, a man ran from behind where an audacious yacht was docked, sprinting away from the looming death-ship. Like a fire extinguisher with an extraordinary range, a spray of white burst through the air and enveloped the fleeing man. It took only two seconds before the man's body hit the boardwalk, one leg raised in mid-flight. The source of the freezing stream was a figure standing on the dock near the Hawthorne. A woman ran along a parallel pier and the ghoul glanced at her before looking away, letting her flee.

"There he is," the professor said.

"Wait," Lily screamed. "He's going to kill you. Let's get the knife."

"He's got to try," Heather said.

The professor started down the little hill

toward the marina, walking as fast as his aged legs would move. Lily turned to Sam, her face contorted with worry. He shrugged.

"Where is the knife?" Lily asked Heather.

"It's on the table. But-"

Before Heather had finished her sentence, Lily was in a dead run for the open edge of the bridge. She reached the gap and without breaking stride dove into the dark water.

"Lily!" Sam yelled. He and Heather raced to where they could see the young woman swimming for her life across the channel.

"Let her go," Heather said. "Maybe she'll get away."

"She's going to get the knife," Sam protested.

"I know. By the time she gets back, the professor should have ended all this." She looked at the old professor's back as he neared the closest pier. "One way or another."

Lily reached the other side of the bridge and climbed the girders up to the lower level where she could take off running. She'd always hated track in school, but it was mostly because it was in school, where kids made fun of her. Now she hated the fact that she wasn't in very good shape. It was a long run to Heather's house. When she got there, she'd be wiped out, and she still had to get back. At least that would be downhill.

When Lily arrived at Heather's house, she found the side door unlocked. Fighting to catch her breath, she walked in and began her desperate search. As Heather had said, she found the knife laying on the kitchen table. The girl stared at the old dagger as her breathing recovered, wondering about its strange power and why some ghoul needed it. It occurred to her then that it looked like something out of an old murder mystery. She grabbed the knife by the handle and turned to start the long run back down to the channel.

Then the darkness closed in and she was falling.

Sam? Yes, but no. He looked like Sam. Jake...no. She could see now it wasn't Jake, just a man who bore a striking resemblance. The body of the man who looked like Jake slid in the water as the ship pitched in the storm and water crashed over the side.

"Krause! What the hell is wrong with you?" *It was the man who looked like Sam.* "Give me my knife."

"There isn't room for all of us up there, Halvorsen. Just me," *Fitch Krause yelled through the blowing wind. He held tight to the mast as rising water swirled around his feet.*

"Please," Halvorsen said. "We'll both fit. Drop the knife and let's get up there before it's too late." *He pointed up the mast into the gray and white blowing snow and rain.*

Krause stuck the knife between his belt and trousers. "Fine. Hurry up," *he said. He motioned for Halvorsen to ascend the swaying mast. Halvorsen jumped to the mast and reached up to grab a ladder rung. As his arm was stretched upward, Krause pulled the knife and plunged it into Halvorsen's side, over and over again. Halvorsen collapsed down to the deck, his arms reaching toward Krause and his mouth moving without sound. Fierce anger and pain distorting his features.*

Finally, words whispered out, "Damn you, Krause." *Then his face sunk below the rising surface, the life leaving his body before the deck disappeared beneath the frigid Lake Superior water.*

Krause scrambled up the mast, the water licking at his feet and legs as the foundered ship finally settled to the bottom. Only ten feet of mast remained above the water, and the swells powered by the storm reached up and soaked Krause's lower body. Still, he clung to his life perch, shivering.

Then out of the clouds and snow a dark shape appeared. A ship, only a hundred yards distant. Krause started shouting for all he was worth. Any captain, on seeing his plight, would launch a dingy to rescue him. He screamed for help and saw first one, then a half-dozen shapes come to the rail. But the ship, one of the steamers, didn't stop or even slow down. Instead, it cruised past, a crowd of men on its deck, staring out at him. As it moved on, the vessel's name came into view, printed in big gold lettering: Melville.

In a final act of rage Krause threw the dagger at the disappearing ship.

The last thing Lily saw was from within the clear depths of Lake Superior; Halvorsen's accusing eyes lifted to Krause's frozen body clinging to a mast and yard that easily could have accommodated three.

"I assume you were known as Fitch Krause, Second Mate, the Hawthorne, lost on fifteen November, eighteen-hundred-eighty-six," the professor said. The remnant of a man that stood before him on the pier chilled him to his soul on appearance alone. Clinging to a desire to right a wrong committed long ago, by other men, the professor choked down the fear that rose like flood waters in his throat. "Fitch Krause. Left to freeze to death on the mast of his foundered ship. Left by my ancestor, Heikki Pekkonen, Captain of the Melville."

Krause's pale eyes narrowed as they bore through the professor. "Go on." The voice was venomous and raspy.

The professor swallowed hard, trying to meet the apparition's gaze. "Mr. Krause, what you endured must have been awful. But my great-great-grandfather did not make that decision lightly. The Melville was bringing medicine to Houghton to save many lives, and he feared risking the ship in the storm. I've read his journal and, for what it's worth, I can tell you it anguished him to leave you behind. It tormented him until his death, as it did his crew."

Krause turned his head, looking up the little hill to where Sam and Heather stood.

"On behalf of Heikki Pekkonen," the professor said, drawing Krause's attention, "Captain of the Melville, from whom I am descended and with whose authority I speak, I now respectfully apologize for the wrong committed against you and ask that you leave this community in peace, knowing that your story will be told in full so that all who now live will know what happened to you."

Krause's face hardened and his eyes took on new energy, silencing the professor and leaving him motionless.

"I'll take your apology and your life, Pekkonen," Krause said. Then he lifted one palm toward the professor and the air around the old professor lost any semblance of warmth. The professor felt the water in his living tissue turn to ice and the blood stop pulsing through his veins. Then he felt nothing.

"No!" Heather screamed.

Sam grabbed her arm, worried she might run down and try to fight Krause, but he felt the strength leave her when Krause turned his malevolent stare upon them. Together they watched the worn and battered body of the sailor as he walked to the gangplank of his decrepit ship. When he reached the deck, Krause turned once more to face them and smiled. Then the fog began to swirl around him and he disappeared. With a loud snap, the sails filled with air and the Hawthorne made an impossibly sharp turn and headed back east through the channel.

Sam let his gaze wander to where Professor Grant Pekkonen stood, frozen in place on the pier.

"He did it," Sam said.

Heather looked at the professor who'd given himself so the rest of the community could live. She heaved a long sigh. "I thought maybe he was going to get to live, when Krause didn't kill him immediately."

"Uh," Sam uttered. He was looking down at the marina. "I see five more bodies down there, besides the professor's."

Heather visibly deflated. Then her head snapped up and she started looking around, a mother duck missing a duckling. "I hope Lily's okay. I haven't seen her."

Sam had been watching for the young lady and hadn't seen her come back to the water's edge. "I think she was gone during all this. She should be all right." But Heather's sudden concern penetrated his spirit. He'd brought her out here and she was his responsibility. Now she was nowhere in sight. He wouldn't be able to relax until they found her. She was on the other side of the channel and he wanted to get over there without hesitation.

Sam looked up at the lift-bridge. "I wonder when that will thaw out enough so they can lower it?"

Heather queried, "Why is it still frozen?"

CHAPTER THIRTEEN

After her episode, Lily realized what needed to be done. She ran directly to Jake's house and stumbled to a halt. The front edge of the door, which was slightly ajar, and the door jamb were white. Frost. Holding the knife in front of her, though she knew it was useless, she crept up to peer through the open gap. A metallic stench assailed her, emanating from inside the house. Blood? No, no, no! She couldn't be too late. Switching the dagger to her left hand she gave the big oak door a feeble push, not really wanting to see inside. The daylight swept across the floor, illuminating first the feet, then the rest of Jake's body where it lay in a big puddle of his own blood. Her heart lurched in her chest and her knees gave out, dropping her onto the front porch, leaving her looking like a penitent sinner begging for mercy. Tears stung her eyes, running down her cheeks, as she considered the one boy in school who might have been nice to her. She could have warned him, if she'd deciphered her visions sooner. Here was Jake, his body slashed and hammered, the victim of an evil that had come back to life seeking unjustified vengeance.

A feeble hope kindled to life and she raised her head. Standing up she stepped into the foyer, averting her eyes from Jake's broken form.

"Mr. Henderson," she called.

There was no response. Not that she really expected one, but she hoped. "Mr. Henderson! Are you home?"

Nothing.

She looked up the broad staircase, somehow feeling she needed to ascend. Just to be sure. Climbing to the second floor was like mounting Everest; her lungs burned and her legs felt like they each weighed a hundred pounds.

Finally, in the hallway, she saw the destroyed door and somehow glided over to it. Inside the room she saw Mr. and Mrs. Henderson huddled together in death, blood everywhere.

Then the vision pierced her mind, tearing her from her despondence. She was wasting time. There was still hope, but she had to get back to the marina.

Bursting from the front door she spied Jake's bike and jumped on. She flew down the hill, doing everything in her power to keep from losing control and pitching into an abrasive wipeout. Tears salted her cheeks, shed for the only boy in school who had shown her any kindness. She gripped the old sailor's knife against the handlebars, the blade sticking up at an awkward angle. She'd be a strange sight for anyone who noticed her flying pell-mell down the street with a big dagger in her hand. Someone might even call the cops.

But she couldn't worry about that. Grant was certainly going to die if he approached Fitch Krause. Krause had a secret to keep and an apology wasn't going to put an end to his killing. Even Professor Pekkonen's death wasn't going to stop him. But this knife might.

Her visions revealed more than what she saw or heard. There was also what she felt. She felt, with vivid acuteness, the emotions and thoughts of those who appeared to her. It was something that was hard to explain to others, so she had never tried. In the moments the Melville was sailing away, Krause had felt not only anger, but fear and regret. If there were three men on that mast, would the captain have risked a rescue then?

The secret that knife possessed had held Krause within his watery grave, unable to rest. But when it was removed, so was his prison. Instead of using his chance to make amends for his treachery, he chose to extract revenge against a captain and crew who had made a difficult choice to ensure they could save a whole population. And he decided to eliminate the descendants of those who could reveal his dark nature. With Jake and his father dead, there was only one man left alive who could use that knife to send Krause to his ultimate judgment.

"Sam!" Lily's voice echoed across the clearing channel. Sam and Heather saw her racing to the water's edge on the far side, the knife clearly in her grasp. She dove into the water and started swimming over. She wasn't even half-way when the water turned gray and a cold wind gusted in from the east. With it came the Hawthorne, sails fully engorged with wind of the ship's own making, cruising directly at the girl.

"Hurry!" Sam screamed. There was no way she was going to make it.

"Lily!" Heather yelled.

Then the battered hull of the ghost ship blocked Lily from view, its deck just slightly higher than where Sam and Heather stood on the bridge's bottom tier. The Hawthorne stopped like it had dropped anchors both fore and aft. Sam saw Krause's back as he moved to the far deck-rail and jumped over the side.

A scream.

Heather grabbed Sam's arm, her face pinched and her eyes watery. Sam didn't know what to do. Didn't know what he *could* do.

Krause re-appeared on the far side of the deck. Lily was bound by a rope that pinned her arms to her sides. Krause raised a gnarled hand, the old dagger in his grip. With his free hand he grabbed Lily by the back of the neck and walked her over to the near rail where Sam and Heather could see her clearly.

"You have to stab him, Sam," she shrieked. "Use the knife. Only you-"

Krause cracked her across the mouth with a rotting fist, silencing the girl and drawing a small stream of blood from her lips.

"Leave her alone," Heather cried. She looked about ready to jump across the ten-foot span of water to the ship's deck and throttle Krause. Now Sam held her arm. If Krause had wanted them dead, he would have simply frozen them to the dock where they stood. Yet here they were.

"Yes, Halvorsen," Krause taunted, his voice oozing through the air like a toxic cloud. "Why don't you come over here and stab me with your knife?" He stabbed the dagger into the rail in front of him. His bright, blue eyes pulsed, full of hate, weakening Sam's knees. "After all, it's *your* knife."

Sam glanced at Heather who returned the look and gave a subtle shake of her head.

"Does he *want* me to kill him?" he whispered

to her.

"I hope so."

Sam was about to line up for a running jump to the boat's deck when Krause spoke again.

"Or save your little friend. One or the other," the fiend said with a smile. Then he pushed Lily, still tied up, into the unnaturally dark water.

Lily hit the water flat on her back, nearly driving the air from her lungs. Unable to use her arms, she sank deep before getting oriented with her head up. She tried kicking her exhausted legs to lift her to the brighter surface and suck in precious air, but if she was ascending, it wasn't fast enough. She knew that Sam was the only one who could kill Krause, and she wanted him to do it. But he'd rescue her first, right? He wouldn't let her drown. No. Heather needed to save her so Sam could take care of Krause. She finally knew that Krause could only kill them with normal physical means; he couldn't use his power against ones who weren't descended from the Melville. But they didn't know that yet. And with Jake and Mr. Henderson dead, Sam was the only one who could kill Krause. Her lungs hurt so much now. Heather? Sam? Help!

Sam had watched Lily fall, her body in slow motion as it hit the water. Just before she had slipped beneath the surface, he saw her innocent brown eyes, pleading with him to save her. In that moment she looked so much like Maggie, his little sister, wanting to be rescued from the relentless grip of drug addiction. The last time he saw Maggie's eyes, they had been glazed over in death, the victim of an overdose. A victim of his inability to save her.

He wouldn't fail again.

Despite his mediocre swimming skill, he dove after Lily. He opened his eyes and saw her form in the depths, struggling to rise. Sound was a dull rumble and his ears began to ache as he dove deeper, unaccustomed to underwater swimming. He realized with horror that he hadn't thought of what he was going to do once he got to her. All he could do was try to bring her up. He had no way of cutting the ropes that bound her. But he was going to get her to the surface. Or die trying.

"Sam, let me go after-" Heather began. But Sam was already a shimmering shape beneath the water's surface, oblivious to everything else around him. She planned on rescuing Lily so he could go stab Krause. The sweet idiot. Though the young woman hadn't finished her sentence, Lily's message had gotten through. At least to her. Sam was the only one who could kill Krause.

Now he was underwater trying to save Lily.

She wondered then why Krause hadn't turned them to ice in their tracks. She pulled her attention from the rippling water where Sam had disappeared, looking up in time to see Krause diving from the rail of the ship, a satisfied scowl on his face.

What the hell was Krause doing? Confusion fled quickly from the obvious answer: he was going to kill Sam and Lily.

Sam gripped Lily's shoulders and tried to hoist her up. But without a solid brace, he only succeeded in pulling himself down to her level.

The sound of something hitting the water resonated from above, but he didn't have time to worry about it. He had to get an arm around Lily's legs and start swimming up. And he had to do it fast because he was running out of air. Lily must be on the edge of sucking nothing but water into her lungs. He'd just gotten a grip on Lily and started powering upward when he saw the pasty face and then felt the iron grip on his own shoulders, pushing him down.

Krause was going to drown them both.

"Shit!" Heather spat. She eyed the knife, still stuck in the deck rail. Whispering a quick prayer, she took a running leap at the ghost ship. Halfway through the air she could see she wasn't going to make the deck. With a rib-cracking thud, she slammed into the ship's hull and desperately threw her arms over the rail, keeping herself from falling into the water. The wind knocked out of her, she twisted and tugged on the handle of the dagger until it finally came free. Air involuntarily rushed back into her empty lungs with a shuddering gasp. Not fully able to breathe she looked down at the water and did the only thing she could think of. She tossed the knife in.

Sam released Lily and fought for his life against an already dead monster. He could see Lily above him now, feebly kicking her legs. Krause seemed to relax, maintaining his grip on Sam's shoulders, satisfied to hold him there indefinitely. Which of course would not have to be much longer. Sam tried to break away so he could propel himself to the surface, but there was no escaping Krause's control. His lungs burned, screaming for him to breathe.

Then something flickered in the water above them and Krause jerked, one hand releasing Sam to grasp at something tumbling through the space between their bodies. His reflexes taking over, Sam crossed his arms out in front of himself, as if to catch a heavy ball against his chest. But what landed in his arms was steely and sharp. He recognized the knife Heather had brought up from her dive and took it by its handle.

Krause let go of Sam and flung himself toward the surface, frantic to get away. But Sam slashed out with the knife, eliciting a bubbling scream of pain and fear from Krause that hammered his eardrums. Sam kicked to get closer to a twitching Krause, still struggling to flee from Sam and the knife. With his free hand Sam grabbed one of Krause's legs and tugged him closer, then repeatedly drove the dagger into the living corpse's side.

Having pulled herself over the rail, Heather looked down at the water hoping that somehow, against the odds, she'd see Sam and Lily's heads break the surface. But there was nothing.

She labored to catch her breath, thinking she would have to dive in and help.

A wail of anguish boomed from the depths, launching forth with such force she thought the water would explode all around her.

But the surface remained calm.

Sam could see Krause's body quit moving. Not knowing or caring if he was truly dead, he swam up to where Lily still struggled. He slipped the knife between her body and the ropes and they fell away as though they wanted to be cut. Her body shot upward.

He kicked once, twice, straining to reach the surface and pull in life-saving air. But with the surface several feet above, his limbs went numb and darkness closed in.

Heather saw something emerging through the clear, dark water. A face. Lily's head burst upward and she sucked in a huge gasp of air. The young woman began treading water, trying to catch her breath.

Heather stumbled as the ship began to shake and rattle beneath her, pieces falling off as it crashed in on itself and water rushed into its lower holds. The rail Heather leaned against instantly felt mushy and weak, disintegrating under her hand. A rancid odor issued from the bowels of the ship, the fetid reek of its death.

"Sam?" Heather shouted.

Lily shook her head and pointed downward, still unable to speak.

Finally, able to breathe normally, Heather took a deep breath and dove into the water.

CHAPTER FOURTEEN

Heather dragged Sam's limp body toward shore where Lily charged back into the water and helped her drag Sam. Once on dry land, Heather checked to see if he was breathing. She raised a face full of concern to Lily and compressed his chest once. Water gurgled out of his open mouth. She felt for his pulse and was relieved to feel a slow, yet present, throb in the carotid artery in his neck. But he still wasn't breathing.

"Do CPR!" Lily shrieked.

Heather placed her mouth over Sam's and blew in a breath. She felt the air go in against resistance and then she pulled back as his body heaved, coughing water out of his lungs.

"Come on, Sam," she said. She shook his body like a frightened child waking a sleeping parent on a night filled with bad dreams. More coughing and he rolled onto his side, sucking in breaths between fits of spewing out water and phlegm. Heather saw his eyes open and stare, unfocused on the ground before his face, his head hanging limp in exhaustion.

"Sam," Lily fell forward and hugged him

from behind.

"Oh, thank God," Heather said. She crawled around in front of him and caressed his shoulder. "Are you okay?"

Slowly, Sam nodded and looked up at her. His eyes were bloodshot and he looked completely spent. "Thanks."

"He's gone," Heather said.

"Only because you two got me the knife." He sat up and peeled Lily off his back and patted her hand with a smile. "I heard what you said. How did you know what to do?"

Lily looked from Sam to Heather and back again. "When I touched the knife, I had another vision. Krause killed your great-great-grandfather. Jake's too." She paused and tears filled her eyes, then cascaded down her round cheeks. "He killed Jake and his parents."

"Oh, honey," Heather said and embraced the girl, fighting tears of her own.

Sniffling, Lily finally pulled away. "Krause stabbed your ancestors on the deck of the Hawthorne as it was sinking because he wanted to go up on the mast himself. He didn't think there was room for three. He used that knife."

Sam sat quietly. Then he said, "I wonder if the Melville would have risked a rescue attempt if there had been three men on that mast?"

A grim smile from Lily. "Krause wondered that too."

Then he looked over at Heather and a grin creased his lips. "You know that dagger just about landed in my arms?"

Heather smiled back. "Doesn't seem like an accident, does it? Maybe it had help."

"Maybe." Sam's brow furrowed and his mouth puckered into a frown. "Why didn't Krause just freeze us, like everyone else?"

"He couldn't," Lily stated. "He could only use his dark magic against those descended from sailors on the Melville. Anyone else, he needed to kill with normal means."

"Like drowning," Heather said.

"Or other things," Lily said, tears trickling once again for Jake. Heather rubbed her shoulders and let her grieve.

When it seemed that Lily had settled down Sam staggered to his feet and tested his balance. Satisfied he could stand and walk, the three walked down to pay their respects to Dr. Grant Pekkonen, a morose silence enveloping them.

A loud crack reverberated down from above, the ice that had disabled the lift-bridge quickly melting and weak now that the Hawthorne was gone. With a rumbling squeal, the deck broke free of its frozen lock, sending splinters of ice tumbling into the water. When it finally settled into place, traffic started to flow in both directions, emergency vehicles descending on the marina.

The dripping trio walked back to Sam's truck and he suddenly stopped. He turned a very serious face on Heather and said, "Do you want to grab some dinner tonight?"

Lily tried to conceal a grin.

Heather tilted her head to the side and looked Sam in the eye. "Naw. But you're welcome to come over for pizza."

Sam chuckled. "Sounds good."

They climbed into the cab of the truck, Lily wedged in between.

"Ms. Case?" Lily said.

"Yes?"

"Please don't ever go wreck diving again."

The End

Also available by Matthew Hellman:

Novel: Solomon's Seal

Short Story: My Nameless Beast (part of the anthology: Six Guns Straight from Hell Vol. 3, Sept. 2020)

For news on upcoming works by Matthew Hellman, visit matthewhellmanauthor.com

Facebook:
https://www.facebook.com/matthew.hellman.7549

Instagram:
https://www.instagram.com/mhellmanauthor/